TwistAPlot® **14**

Instant Millionaire

R.L. Stine

Illustrations by Jowill Woodman

D0596484

SCHOLASTIC INC.
New York Toronto London Auckland Sydney Tokyo

ISBN 0-590-33231-7

Copyright © 1984 by Robert Stine. All rights reserved. Published by Scholastic Inc. by arrangement with Parachute Press, Inc.

12 11 10 9 8 7 6 5 4 3   5 6 7 8/8

DO YOU FEEL LUCKY TODAY?

If you do, turn the page and enter the lottery! YOU may be a winner and become an INSTANT MILLIONAIRE!

If you win the grand prize, you have one month to spend it all or give it all away. If you *can't* get rid of the million dollars in one month, you must give the unspent money back and you'll lose out on an even bigger fortune.

Think it will be easy to get rid of a million dollars? Think it will be fun???

It will all depend on the choices you make. By following the directions at the bottom of each page, YOU will decide what to do with the money.

If you make the right choices, you might end up with a fortune in cash! If you make the wrong choices, you may have to beg your parents for a million dollar advance on your allowance!

To enter the lottery, turn to PAGE 2.

Are you ready to enter the INSTANT MILLIONAIRE lottery?

Who knows? You might be the grand-prize winner and find yourself with a million dollars in cash! (That, plus the money you make from babysitting, should put you in pretty good shape, don't you think?)

Pick a number — any one of these four: 7, 13, 25, or 50. One of these numbers will win you the grand prize — and set you off on a bookful of adventures.

Which number do you choose?

Number 7? Turn to PAGE 10.
Number 13? Turn to PAGE 75.
Number 25? Turn to PAGE 26.
Number 50? Turn to PAGE 30.

Good luck!

"Pull over, Cummings!" you tell your chauffeur. He pulls the big red Cadillac limo to the curb.

You're on your way home from a long day of shopping, and you've just spotted five or six of your friends at the playground. "Hey, Andy! Jack!" you call.

They look up, but they don't seem to recognize you. "They probably can't imagine who would be calling to them from a big limo," you tell yourself. You jump out of the car. "Hey, guys—it's me!"

They give you a little wave and go back to their conversation.

"Wait here for me, Cummings," you tell your driver. You go running up to your friends on the baseball diamond.

"Hi, Andy. Hi, Jack. Hi, everyone. I haven't seen you guys for a while. I've been busy shopping."

"Yeah, we heard," Andy says.

Something is wrong. These are your best friends—and they're not acting too friendly.

What's going on?

Turn to PAGE 29.

4

"Okay. Hand it over," he says slowly. "I know this is a gag. But I'll bite."

He takes the ten thousand dollar bills from your hand and examines the money carefully. "Okay. What's the joke?" he asks.

"No joke," you tell him. "It's yours."

"Hey—Frank, whatcha doin'?" A boy in a sweatshirt and torn jeans comes over.

"This kid just gave me ten thousand dollars," Frank says. "It even looks real!"

"Hey, kid—you got some more of that for me?" Frank's friend asks.

"Sure," you say. "Here's ten thousand for you." Business is starting to pick up!

"Hey—this kid's giving away money!" Frank's friend yells to two other teenagers. They come running over. You dig into your pocket for more money.

A few seconds later, a huge crowd has gathered around you. You're handing out the thousand dollar bills as fast as you can. But it isn't fast enough! Hands are grabbing at you. A fist fight breaks out. You hear a window smash, broken glass shattering against the floor. People are scuffling, pushing their way toward you.

You've started a terrible, violent riot! Should you try to run away?—or stay until you've given away every dollar you brought?

Run? Turn to PAGE 9.
Stay? Turn to PAGE 19.

A strangely dressed little man knocks at your front door. He's wearing a long, black frock coat and a black derby hat. He's carrying an ebony walking stick in one hand and a long, narrow box in the other.

"I'm pleased to make your acquaintance," he says in a clipped British accent. "I represent the mysterious millionaire Otto Quincy Vandermint, III."

"Otto Quincy Vandermint, III?" you ask.

"Well, we *think* that's his name," the little man says. "We're not sure really. His name might be Bob Johnson. His handwriting is very hard to decipher."

You usher him into the living room and offer him a seat. "No, thank you," he says. "I never sit. It's bad for the circulation."

He puts down his walking stick and holds up the long, narrow box. "Mister Vandermint—or Mister Johnson, whichever it is—has informed me that you are the grand-prize winner in the Instant Millionaire Lottery, which he sponsors. He has asked me to give you this box containing one million dollars in cash."

"Gulp!" That's all you manage to say.

"I'll pass that along to Mister Vandermint," the little man says. "Before I hand over the money to you, I have a document here that you must read. You knew there had to be a catch to this—didn't you?"

Go on to PAGE 7.

The little man hands you a sheet of paper and stands watching as you read the typewritten message it contains:

Dear INSTANT MILLIONAIRE:

I am handing over to you as grand-prize winner the sum of one million dollars. You must abide by the following rules:

1. You have one month to spend all of the money.

2. You must spend it yourself. No one else can help you.

3. If you manage to spend the million dollars within one month, you shall receive five million dollars more. You may do whatever you please with this five million.

4. You cannot gamble with the money or use it in any illegal manner.

5. You can give the money away—but not to anyone you know.

6. If you *cannot* spend or give away the million dollars in one month, you must return all unspent money to me. And you forfeit the additional five million.

You struggle to read the signature at the bottom of the page, but you can't make it out.

"Will you agree to these rules?" the little man asks.

Go on to PAGE 8.

"You bet!" you cry, sounding more excited than you'd expected. You reach out to shake hands.

"I'm sorry. I never shake hands. Bad for the skin," the little man says. "Here. Take this box, please. It's quite heavy."

He hands you the box containing the million dollars. "Thank you!" you cry. You place the box on the coffee table.

The man picks up his walking stick. "I'll show myself out," he says. He turns and walks into the coat closet.

"Maybe *I'd* better show you out," you say, leading him toward the front door.

"Enjoy your prize," he says, walking quickly down the street. "And don't spend it all in one place! Hahahaha!"

You close the door and carry the box into your room. "If only Uncle Clyde were home!" you tell yourself. "I've just *gotta* tell someone about this!" You open the box. The money is in one thousand dollar bills! You close the box and hide it in the back of your sock drawer.

You decide to run over and see your friend Andy. You've got to tell him about your lottery prize! You lock the front door carefully behind you. You turn the corner and begin to walk down Andy's street.

Wait a minute! That man back there—is he *following* you???

Turn to PAGE 37.

"I've gotta get out of here!" you tell yourself, ducking away from someone's fist.

You start to run. But you are trapped inside a circle of fighting, struggling people. You cannot get out. You have no choice but to stay and see this whole mess through to the bitter end.

Keep handing out those thousand dollar bills—and turn to PAGE 19.

CONGRATULATIONS!!!

You picked number 7—and number 7 is a $100,000 winner!

Unfortunately, number 7 is a very popular number in instant money lotteries. It's so popular that 100,000 people picked number 7.

This means that you must share your prize with 99,999 others. That leaves you with exactly one dollar.

After taxes, your prize is about fifty cents.

When you deduct the price of this book from that amount, you owe us money!

Please don't send cash through the mail. A check or money order will do.

THE END

The party isn't supposed to start until noon, but people begin arriving at eight in the morning. It's a windy, gray day. You peer out of the communications tent you set up and hope that it doesn't rain.

Bands begin to play. People are taking tickets for the lottery of the thousand Cadillac door prizes. Hundreds of helium balloons float over the park, bright colors against the darkening sky.

"Won't be much fun if it rains," Uncle Clyde says, his usual cheerful self.

The phone rings. He picks it up for you. He talks for a while, then comes over to see you. "Bad news," he says, shaking his head.

What could go wrong now?

JOHN L. WOODMAN

Turn to PAGE 39.

Your Uncle Clyde comes home at six, and you run to the front door to greet him. "My million dollars came today!" you shout excitedly.

"Good," he says, putting down his cap and newspaper on the coffee table. "Anything else new?"

You knew he'd be as nonchalant as ever. It would take more than a million dollars to get Uncle Clyde excited.

"Some newspaper people were here a few minutes ago to take my picture for *The Gazette,*" you tell him, following him into the kitchen.

"I don't read *The Gazette,*" Uncle Clyde says, opening the refrigerator, "and trouble is money. Do you know what I mean by that?"

"No," you say.

"Listen, can you lend me a twenty till Friday?" he asks.

"No," you reply. "According to the rules, I can't give any of it to anyone I know."

"Well, then, it's not much good, is it?"

Go on to PAGE 13.

"I have to spend it all or give it away in one month," you tell him. "If I can do that, I get five million dollars more."

He takes out some lettuce and a tomato. "I hope you don't get a swelled head from this," he says, looking for the white bread. "I imagine once you get five million dollars, there'll no talkin' to you."

"Well, I don't have it yet," you say. "First I have to decide how I'm going to get rid of this million."

This is a big decision! Are you going to try to spend it all? Or are you going to try to give the million dollars away?

Spend it? Turn to PAGE 42.
Give it away? Turn to PAGE 50.

You settle back in your airplane seat and prepare for takeoff. Uncle Clyde, seated beside you, has his head buried in a newspaper, as usual. "He's going to be as much fun as ever," you tell yourself.

But there's no way that Uncle Clyde is going to get you down. Here you are, about to go on a trip around the world—with a million dollars to spend! (Well, a little less than a million. It took a couple hundred thousand to rent the private jet you're about to take off in!)

The plane takes off. You watch the town grow smaller and smaller beneath you. The pilot heads the big jet toward the south. "Rio de Janeiro, here we come!" you cry.

"Not so loud. I'm trying to read," scolds Uncle Clyde.

"I can't wait to see Brazil," you tell him. "It must be really beautiful!"

Several hours later, you are landing in Rio. You ride by the beautiful, golden beaches on the way to your hotel. "Looks pretty crowded," mutters Uncle Clyde.

You arrive at the hotel and go up to the desk to register. "Are you the young lottery winner we've read about in the newspapers?" the clerk asks. You answer that you are. "Well, enjoy your stay. Everything is on the house!" he declares. "Good publicity, you know!"

Go on to PAGE 15.

"The hotel has a guided tour down the Amazon!" you tell your uncle after a few days of soaking up the sun on Rio's beaches. "It costs a hundred thousand dollars per person, plus tips. Let's do it!"

"Well . . . okay," Uncle Clyde agrees. "But there might be flies on that river."

The next morning, you meet the tour guide. "Let me pay you in advance," you tell him.

"Pay me? Oh no!" the tour guide cries, horrified at the thought. "You are my guests. For you, famous North American lottery winners, the tour shall be free! Please do not insult me by offering me money!"

The tour of the Amazon takes a week. Sailing down the wide, purple river, you see sights you will never forget. "Now we'd better fly to Europe where we can spend some money," you tell your uncle upon your return. "Time is getting short."

You fly your private jet to London and check in at a tiny, exclusive hotel near Buckingham Palace. "The American lottery winner has arrived!" cries the delighted hotel owner. "Please—enjoy your stay at our humble hotel for free! You are our guests!"

Will you ever be able to spend your money?

Turn to PAGE 36.

JOWILL WOODMAN

You are standing on the deck, staring at the ice. You are cold and hungry. Food is running out, and so the captain is serving only one meal a day. Strong winds begin to batter the ship. There appears to be another storm on the horizon.

You turn to go back to your cabin. You couldn't be more depressed. Today is the last day of the month, your last day to spend the million dollars. Your last day in this lifetime to be a millionaire!

"How's it goin'?" a voice asks.

You look up to see the captain.

"I'm sorry I ever bought this ship," the captain mutters. "It's been nothing but trouble. And now look where it's got me, stuck in the middle of the ocean, with a thousand hungry, furious passengers aboard."

"I'll give you a million dollars for the ship," you say.

"Sold," he says. The two of you shake hands.

A driving rain begins to batter the ship. The wind roars through the deck, shattering portholes. People scream in terror as the ship lurches up, then down.

"My lucky day!" you cry joyously. "What a lucky day!!"

THE END

You turn around. You are on the highway heading back to town now. All of your attempts to slow the car have brought it down to only 55 m.p.h.!

You see an empty field filled with tall grass. Maybe the tall grass will slow the car. You pull into the field, steering over the bumps and through the grass that comes up over your low windshield.

After a few terrifying, bumpy minutes, the racing car finally slows, then comes to a stop.

Your heart is still racing as you walk the two miles into town. You are extremely angry by the time you get back to the car showroom. You are determined to give that salesman a piece of your mind. He had no business sending you out in a car without brakes!

"Is that the kind of merchandise you sell?" you scream, bursting into his office. "What kind of a place is this that sells cars without brakes? I could've been killed! That car is a piece of junk! Just junk!" The salesman backs away, horrified. "How much does that car sell for, anyway?" you ask, your eyes filled with fury.

"It sells for half a million dollars," he says, his voice shaking.

"Oh. I see. Well, in that case I'll take *two* of them!" you say. "Where do I sign?"

THE END

"The money is all gone! It's all gone!" you scream as loudly as you can.

But the fighting continues for several minutes more. It takes approaching police sirens to get the crowd to stop struggling. The sirens grow louder. The fighting stops. People quickly walk away, leaving you standing in front of the shattered windowglass of the store.

You look around at the broken windows, empty display windows, and trash and rubble strewn all about the area. "Here's the person who started it, officer!" you hear a voice call. A tall policeman is walking quickly toward you.

You realize that you have successfully given away half of the million dollars. But you don't care. This is the worst day of your life. And now you are about to be arrested.

Can things get any worse??

Turn to PAGE 27.

"Can I give someone ten thousand dollars?" you ask, holding the money up so that everyone who passes by can see it. But everyone continues to pass by—nobody stops.

Your arm is getting tired from holding up the money. "Free ten thousand dollars here!" you shout.

"These kids!" a woman says to a companion as they walk by you. "They just don't know what to do with themselves in the summertime."

Her companion, a tall woman in bright green slacks and top, stops to look at you. "What are you selling there?" she asks.

"I'm not selling anything," you say. "I'm trying to give away ten thousand dollars. Would you like it?" You hold the money out to her.

She takes a step back. "Why don't you go to the library and see if you can find a nice book to read?" she asks, and she and her friend go into the store.

"Hey, can you spare a quarter?" You feel a hand tugging at your sleeve. It's a disheveled-looking man in filthy, ragged clothes.

Is this your big opportunity to give away some money?

Go on to PAGE 21.

"I don't have a quarter. Take ten thousand dollars," you tell him, thrusting the money into his dirty hand.

"Give me a break," the bum mutters, pushing the money back at you. He starts to walk away. "Can't make a decent living begging anymore," he says, shaking his head. "Too many creeps and weirdos!"

Shoppers continue to walk right by you. "I have an honest face," you tell yourself. "Why doesn't anyone believe me?"

Should you try a different location in the mall? Or should you go home and think up a better plan for giving away the million?

A different location? Turn to PAGE 64.
Go home and think of a new plan? Turn to PAGE 92.

"Well," you tell yourself, "shopping is bound to be a lot more fun when you have a million dollars to spend!"

You crinkle a few thousand dollar bills between your fingers. It's hard to believe that these insignificant pieces of paper can make a person feel so powerful ... so ... RICH!

What shall you spend the million dollars on?

The first thing that comes to mind is chocolate bars. But you realize that there probably isn't a million dollars' worth of chocolate bars to be bought in your town. Besides, where would you keep them? You could probably eat only a few thousand dollars' worth the first day. You'd have to store the rest somewhere.

"No," you tell yourself, "chocolate bars are out." You have to buy something expensive. You have to spend your million on cars—or diamonds. (Then you can spend your next five million on chocolate bars!)

So—which will it be?

Cars? Turn to PAGE 31.
Diamonds? Turn to PAGE 40.

ZZZZZZZZZZZZZZAAAAAAAAP!

It would have been smarter to show them your money.

Beside dictionaries inside their pouches, the creatures also carry blaster ray guns—as you've just discovered.

You've also just discovered that these creatures get a bit impatient if someone should happen to say no to them.

In your case, they became impatient enough to blast you to smithereens.

Since you are now a fine, gray powder settling over the sidewalk, you probably realize that this adventure has come to . . .

THE END

"After five centuries, the diamond is ours again," the man holding the blowgun says to his comrades. "After five centuries of being deprived of its beauty, our nation shall enjoy it once more, this national treasure restored thanks to our efforts."

"And what of this person?" one of the others says, gesturing toward you. "This unfortunate soul has learned too much about us."

The men continue to gaze at their newly regained treasure. The diamond seems to hypnotize them. No one answers the man who spoke about you.

You decide that you'd better try to escape while they are still transfixed by the diamond. If you can get out to the forest, you can surely lose them.

But should you try to make a grab for the diamond? Or should you just run for your life and leave the diamond behind?

Decide quickly.

Grab for the diamond as you try to escape? Turn to PAGE 32.

Simply run for your life? Turn to PAGE 73.

You don't look back.

You just start running.

You grab the shopping bag with the diamond inside—and you run, faster than you've ever run before.

"They must be after the diamond," you tell yourself. "They followed me from the jewelry store!"

WHISSSSSSSH!

You run into the small woods beside your neighbor's house. You know there's no way you can lose them. Should you hide the diamond? You can hide it inside the hollow tree by the wild rose bushes.

But, if they catch you *without* the diamond—what will they do to you? You might be safer if you keep the diamond with you.

You must decide fast. Hide the diamond—or keep running with it?

Hide it? Turn to PAGE 62.
Keep running with it? Turn to PAGE 51.

CONGRATULATIONS!!!

You picked number 25—and number 25 is the grand-prize winner!

That's right! You've won a million dollars in cash!!

Now all you have to do is hand in your lottery ticket.

Where is it? Not in that pocket? Try the other pocket. No?

How about your wallet? Did you put it in your wallet?

It's yellow, bright yellow. You can't mistake it for anything else. Keep looking. How about your dresser? Did you put it in one of the drawers? No? Did you put it in one of your textbooks? In your notebook? No?

Keep looking! Keep looking! You can't give up! You *can't!*

Look everywhere. Under the bed. Under the sink. Behind the couch. In the dog's dish.

No? You can't find it??

What a disappointment.

Oh, well. Maybe you'll win a million dollars some other time. Those are the breaks, right?

THE END

Uncle Clyde shows up at the police station two hours later. "I would've been here sooner," he apologizes, "but I was watching a good movie on TV."

The police officer explains to Uncle Clyde what happened at the mall. You're so embarrassed and ashamed, you wish you could slip through a crack in the floor. Here you are, halfway toward your goal of giving away the million dollars, and you've never felt more miserable.

The phone rings. "This is probably the manager of the mall," the policeman says. "He's calling to say what the damages came to."

The policeman talks on the phone for a few minutes. Then he hangs up and turns to you and your uncle. "The damages at the mall come to half a million dollars," he says sternly. He gives you a fierce, angry look. "Do you hear that? You have to pay half a million dollars in damages."

"YAAAAAY!!!" you cry, jumping out of your seat. "I'M RICH! I'M RICH!! YAAAAAAAAY!"

THE END

The teenager staring at the watches turns around as you walk up to him. He's tall and thin, with short red hair. He's wearing a T-shirt that says "Give Me Air."

You decide to get right to the point. "I'm trying to give away some money," you tell him. "I'm not crazy or anything. I just have a lot of money to give away."

The teenager stares at you for a moment. "I'm kinda busy," he says.

"It'll only take a second," you tell him. "Just take some money from me."

"Well . . . if it'll make you happy," the guy says, grinning. "How about five dollars? Have you got a five?"

"I was thinking of a slightly higher amount," you say.

"You mean you want to give away ten dollars?"' the teenager asks. "Are you *sure* you're not crazy?"

"How about a thousand dollars?" you ask, holding up a wad of bills. "Please. I'm serious. I'm giving you ten thousand dollars." You can't believe you have to plead with someone to take the money!

The teenager just stares at you. He's trying to decide if you're serious or not. You hold the money up in front of his face.

Will he take the money? Will he be your first success?

Turn to PAGE 4.

"How you guys doin'?" you ask.

"Fine, fine," they mutter quietly.

"Hey, you know, I bought six arcade games for my room. Want to come over and play them? I've got 'em fixed so you don't have to put any money in."

There's a long silence. "Yeah, maybe sometime," Andy says.

"Listen, anytime you guys want to come to my movie theater, you can get in for free," you offer.

"Thanks," Jack says glumly. He seems really nervous.

"It's nice of a millionaire like you to stop by and say hi," Andy says.

So *that's* what's bothering them!

"Listen, guys, all that money hasn't changed me any," you say. "I'm the same person I was a few weeks ago."

They all look over at your limo and its driver, and shake their heads.

Are your friends right? Has the money changed you? Have you been too selfish by spending all the money on yourself? Should you buy something they can all enjoy? Or do you think you have the right to enjoy spending the money any way you wish? You must decide what to do next.

Keep spending the money as quickly as you can? Turn to PAGE 38.

Spend the money on something everyone can enjoy? Turn to PAGE 54.

30

CONGRATULATIONS!

Number 50 is a winning number!

It isn't the grand-prize-winning number. But you *have* won a jumbo prize.

"Jumbo—Jumbo, come over here, boy!"

That's right! Your very own two-ton elephant.

You'll definitely be the envy of every kid on your block, don't you agree?

Well . . . better go tell the good news to Uncle Clyde. Stock up on peanuts. Buy a big shovel.

And—oh, yes—congratulations again!

THE END

The sign on the fancy car emporium reads: FANCY CAR EMPORIUM.

Inside are the most expensive sport and racing cars in town. At first, the salesman doesn't want to be bothered with you because you are so young. But you wave a few thousand dollar bills under his nose, and his attitude suddenly changes.

"I think you'll be interested in this racing car," he says, leading you to a low, sleek, silver number. "It's perfect for city driving. It goes up to 230 miles per hour and gets four miles to the gallon."

"Sounds good," you say nonchalantly.

"You're not old enough to drive this, are you?" the salesman asks as you slide behind the wheel. You tell him that you're not. "Oh, well, who will know?" he says, handing you the keys. "Go ahead."

You start the powerful engine and drive the car right out the door!

Turn to PAGE 74.

The three men in white robes stand around the small card table, transfixed by the blue-white glow of the diamond—your diamond. They are so overwhelmed by the diamond, they haven't even bothered to tie you up.

You stand up. Do they notice you?

No.

You run toward the card table, reach your hand out, and grab the diamond. "Got it!" you cry aloud.

Now you turn and start to run toward the door.

"Stop!" one of the men yells.

His voice startles you. The diamond slips from your hand. It falls to the floor and . . .

SHATTERS!

"A fake! A fake!" the men are screaming. "It is not a diamond—it is only glass!"

All four of you are frozen where you stand, staring at the pieces of glass on the floor.

Suddenly there is a loud knocking on the cabin door.

Who can that be??

Turn to PAGE 89.

The robed man pulls you back into the cabin. "What are they going to do to me now?" you wonder with terror.

"I'm afraid you've failed the Bonus Round," one of the men says. He removes the long, white hair and long, white beard that hid his face. It is the little man who delivered the million dollars to you.

"We give all of our winners a Bonus Round," the little man explains. The other men remove their white wigs and pack up their belongings. "If you had managed to escape, you would have won a nice prize. It's a little extra opportunity that Otto Quincy Vandermint—if that's his name— likes to give."

You are so relieved, so surprised, so disappointed, so glad, it takes you a while to speak. Finally, you manage to ask, "What would my prize have been?"

"This beautiful ballpoint pen," the little man says. "It's real nifty. It comes with a special clip so you can wear it on your pocket. Too bad, but you'll just have to get by with the five million dollars you won by buying the diamond!"

"Yes, it's too bad," you say. "How could I be so unlucky? I guess that diamond has a curse on it after all!"

You ride home with a big smile on your face, happy this adventure has come to . . .

THE END

Fur-lined gold lamé sneakers
24-speed racing bike
Olympic-sized swimming pool with redwood deck and sauna
Two thoroughbred racehorses with trainers
Chauffeur-driven, cherry-red Cadillac limousine
62 sweaters
62 shirts to match
62 pairs of jeans
A triplex movie theater

That's what you bought on the *first* day of your shopping spree. Of course, you were just getting warmed up. The second day, you did much better!

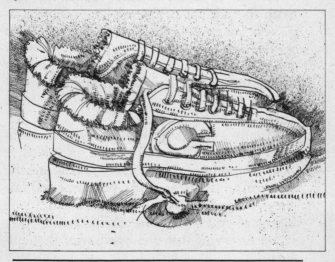

Turn to PAGE 3.

You are treated the same way in Spain, in France, and in Greece. No one will allow "the famous American lottery winner" to spend a dime.

"What am I going to do?" you ask Uncle Clyde. "I have only three days to go, and I still have most of the million dollars!"

"Well . . . we've had a darned nice trip," he says, his face buried in a newspaper. Then he remembers something. "A while back, I read about this ancient monastery high up in the Himalayas. Monks live there untouched by the centuries. I'll bet that's one place where no one has heard of you. Maybe you could donate what's left of your million to the monastery."

"Uncle Clyde, you have come through with the perfect solution!"

You fly to Nepal. You hire sherpas to guide you up the steep, snow-covered mountains. The wind howls, the snow often drifts above your head—but you are determined to reach this secluded monastery that time has forgotten.

Finally, you stagger into the ancient monastery. A hooded monk greets you. "Congratulations!" he cries. "You are the one-millionth person to visit our monastery! Your stay here is our gift to you!" He stares at you from beneath his hood. "Say . . . aren't you the one who won that lottery?!"

THE END

Yes. A man is walking quickly toward you.

He's following you, all right.

Now what should you do?

Andy's house is a block and a half away. Should you make a run for it? What if the man runs after you, follows you there? You don't want to get Andy into danger, too.

Maybe you should turn the corner and head for the school. Summer school is in session, so the building will be open. You can hide in there until the man gives up.

But the school is nearly three blocks away. Andy's house is closer.

Which shall it be?

Decide quickly. The man is getting closer.

Andy's house? Turn to PAGE 55.
The school? Turn to PAGE 84.

You feel bad about your friends. But you quickly decide that they're just jealous. Besides, when they see the arcade games, the swimming pool, and all the other neat stuff you've bought, they'll change their minds and enjoy it with you.

You spend the next day shopping. And the day after that.

The day after that, the little man in the black frock coat is waiting at your front door when you return, your arms full of packages. "Don't worry," you tell him cheerily, "I've almost spent it all."

"That's too bad," he says.

You put your packages down on the walk. "What do you mean?" you ask, fear creeping up your back.

"We've made an unfortunate error," the little man says. "Remember I told you how bad Mr. Vandermint's handwriting is? Well . . . er . . . you see . . . your name doesn't have two sets of double w's—does it?"

"No. Of course not," you reply warily.

"Well, that means we—I mean I—gave the money to the wrong person. We all make mistakes, don't we? I hope it won't be too inconvenient to give everything back."

You slowly, painfully nod your head. You agree to return everything. "Hey— Andy, wait up!" you yell, seeing your friend. "Have I got a story for you!!"

THE END

"Problem with the pizza," Uncle Clyde says mysteriously. He hands you the phone.

The woman's voice at the other end is shaky and apologetic. "I'm so sorry," she says, "but we've made a little mistake with the pizzas. We sent them to the wrong town."

You are too stunned to talk.

"Hello? Hello?" she says. "We must have a bad connection. Anyway, the pizza was sent 300 miles to the south to a little town called Prairieville. I don't know *what* they're going to do with enough pizza for 60,000 people. But they're stuck with it."

"But what about me?" you cry. "What am I supposed to do?"

"Don't worry," the woman says. "You'll receive a full refund. You'll get all your money back!"

Turn to PAGE 91.

You take your box of thousand dollar bills and rush downtown to the fanciest jewelry store in town. You read the name on the shiny silver door: "Diamonds 'n' Stuff."

A tall, distinguished man in a dark-blue suit walks up to greet you. "I'm afraid we don't have a children's department," he says haughtily.

"I'm the million dollar lottery winner," you tell him, holding the money box tightly. "What have you got that costs a million dollars?"

"I think I have a few items you might like," he says, his attitude changing immediately. He disappears into the back of the store to find some diamonds to show you.

"I can't believe this!" you tell yourself. "Is this really me in this incredible store about to buy a million dollar diamond?!"

Is it really this easy to spend a million? You'll soon find out.

Turn to PAGE 58.

"But that's impossible, Officer!" you find yourself saying a few moments later. "This man *can't* be a counterfeiter!"

"Well . . . we think we can prove in court that he is," the policeman says sternly. "He's been telling people that he represents some millionaire who doesn't even exist, and he's been passing out phony thousand dollar bills." He helps his partner push the little man into the squad car. "Hey—what do *you* know about this guy, kid?" the policeman asks.

"Oh . . . uh . . . nothing," you say.

"Nice-looking car you've got there," the other policeman says. "Is that new?"

"Yes," Uncle Clyde replies quietly. "It's . . . uh . . . just borrowed."

He turns the car around and heads back toward the showroom.

"I was an instant millionaire . . ." you say, ". . . for an instant!"

"Well, I have a little money saved up," Uncle Clyde says cheerily. "Maybe we could still afford to get me that Chevy!"

THE END

"I'm going to spend it!" you exclaim. "I'm going to spend a million dollars! That shouldn't be too hard, should it?"

"Easy come, easy go," Uncle Clyde mutters with a mouthful of sandwich.

You ignore his wild enthusiasm. "Now what should I spend it on?"

"I've got a coupla suggestions," he offers, becoming a bit more interested. "You know, your cousin Margaret desperately needs a new freezer. Her ice cream is so soft, she has to drink it. Poor thing."

"Tsk tsk," you say, unsympathetic to poor cousin Margaret's plight.

"And your Uncle Al could use a new car. His is almost five years old!" Uncle Clyde says, chewing with his mouth open.

"Poor Uncle Al. That's real tough," you say.

"I *knew* that money would change you," your uncle says, shaking his head sadly. "Guess you want to spend that whole million on yourself. Well, okay. Go ahead. Buy yourself a million dollar pair of sneakers. Something practical like that."

"I've got an idea!" you cry.

Go on to PAGE 43.

"How big is this town?" you ask.

"About 30,000 people, I guess," Uncle Clyde replies. "Give or take 30,000 or so."

"Great!" you cry. "I'm going to throw a party for everyone in town! The biggest party ever given. A million dollar celebration!"

"Well . . . you'd better vacuum the living room if you're gonna invite 30,000 people over!" Uncle Clyde suggests, still concentrating on his sandwich.

"I'll get rid of the million dollars—and everyone will have the time of their lives!"

"Too hard," your uncle says. "Too complicated. Go buy jewels. Buy cars. Buy stuff like that. Spend the million the easy way. Then throw your party to celebrate."

"Hmmmm . . . I'm a little worried about you, Uncle Clyde. You're beginning to make sense!"

Which idea is better? Go buy jewels, cars, and expensive items? Or throw a million dollar party for your whole town?

If you choose to go buy expensive stuff, turn to PAGE 22.

If you choose to have the big party, turn to PAGE 72.

"I don't believe in ancient curses," you say. "I'll take the diamond."

"You're making a big mistake," the clerk says ominously. "But it's your million dollars. Shall I have it gift-wrapped for you?"

"No, I'll eat it here," you say.

"What?"

"That was just a joke," you tell him. "A very old joke."

"I don't get it," he says. He disappears to wrap up the diamond.

A few minutes later, having spent the million dollars, you are walking home with the diamond in a little shopping bag. You turn the corner onto your block when—WHISSSSSSSH!—something whizzes past your head!

You duck.

You feel it a second time—something whooshes past, narrowly missing you.

Is someone with a blowgun shooting darts at you? Or have you just seen too many movies?

Turn to PAGE 25.

"Money! Money! Money! Money!"

All four heads begin repeating the word over and over. The weird, purple creatures seem to be begging, their eight eyes all pleading as they stare into your eyes.

"Why on earth would these creatures want money?" you ask yourself. "Do they know about my million dollars? Do they just want to see what Earth money looks like?"

"Money! Money!" they cry.

You have to decide whether to show them your money or not.

If you choose to show it to them, turn to PAGE 53.

If you think it would be smarter not to show it to them, turn to PAGE 23.

JOHN WOODMAN

"Let's try the Waterfall Roller Coaster first," Andy says.

"Okay. Good idea," you say, beaming proudly. "Follow me, you guys!" You lead your friends to the entrance to the Waterfall Roller Coaster, where you all climb into the cars that will carry you up to the top of the waterfall.

Up, up, the cars move slowly. "Hey—I've never been on one this tall!" Jack yells from the car behind you.

"Wait till we start to drop!" you scream. "You won't believe it!"

The cars reach the top. Then they stop.

You wait. And wait.

And wait.

"You won't believe it!" you yell again. But it's obvious to everyone that the cars are stuck. You're not going to drop.

"Well . . . uh . . . we sure have a nice view up here, don't we?" you ask, trying to sound cheerful.

Half an hour later, fire trucks arrive. The firemen put up tall ladders and carry everyone down.

"Well, things have got to get better now!" you say cheerfully.

Will they? Turn to PAGE 57.

The woman is trying to pull her young daughter into a shoe store, and the little girl is pulling in the other direction. "Excuse me," you say, walking up behind her.

"YAAAIII!" she cries. It seems that you've startled her. Bad start.

"WAAAAH WAAAAH!" The little girl starts to scream. She is as loud—and as piercing—as an ambulance siren.

"Sorry I startled you," you say to the woman. "I'd like to give you a thousand dollars."

"What?? I can't hear you!" the woman screams, pulling her daughter by the arm, trying to turn her around to comfort her.

"WAAAAAAAH! WAAAAAAH!"

"I just want to give you some money," you say.

"What? You what?!?"

"Money!" you yell. "Money!"

"WAAAAAAAH! WAAAAAAH!"

"I know it's hard for you kids to get summer jobs," the woman says, struggling to pick up her screaming daughter. "But I think you can find *something* better to do than begging!"

"WAAAAAAH! WAAAAAAH!"

The woman walks away, carrying the screaming baby. You turn and see Uncle Clyde approaching. What does *he* want?

Go on to PAGE 49.

"Good news," Uncle Clyde says in his normal, deathlike monotone.

"I'm glad one of us has good news," you say. "What is it?"

"We have to go home and pack. We're leaving tomorrow morning," he tells you, leading you out of the mall.

"What? What are you talking about?"

"I'm being transferred immediately to Wago Wago. It's a tiny island somewhere in the South Seas."

"But—you can't! We can't!" you cry, horrified. "My million dollars! There's no way I could spend a million dollars on a tiny island!"

"They don't even take American money," Uncle Clyde says flatly. "But what can I do? A pipe fitter has to go wherever people need pipes fitted."

"Tomorrow?" you cry.

"It's an emergency pipe fitting. That's why they called me in. They know I'm the best." He suddenly sees how upset you are. "Hey—don't feel bad. We're gonna make out all right on this trip. Since it's a rush job, I'm gonna get time and a half!

THE END

The next morning, you tuck a huge wad of thousand dollar bills into your wallet and take the bus to the nearest shopping mall. You pick a spot in front of Marland's, the most popular department store in the mall. It is only 10:30 in the morning, but there are lots of shoppers coming in and out.

You pull a thousand dollar bill out of your wallet and hold it up. "Can I give someone this thousand dollar bill?" you call out.

No one stops.

"Get your thousand dollar bills right here!" you shout.

Shoppers walk right past you into the store.

"Anyone want a free thousand dollar bill?" you call out.

Twenty minutes later you are still standing there, holding the first thousand dollar bill in your hand. No one has stopped. Very few people have even looked at you!

"I'd better try a different approach," you tell yourself.

Should you offer a larger amount of money? Or should you pick specific people out of the crowd and go up and talk to them personally?

Offer a larger amount? Turn to PAGE 20.
Pick out specific people? Turn to PAGE 78.

You toss the shopping bag away, holding the little box containing the diamond tightly in your hand. You run through the trees, twisting and turning through the woods, trying to lose your pursuers.

Can you outrun them? No. You feel powerful hands grab your shoulders. You feel yourself being lifted up. Have you been captured by a giant?

"I have him. And I believe we have finally regained our precious diamond," a deep voice, the voice of the man holding you captive, calls to his companions.

You cannot see who they are. You are blindfolded and carried to a car. You ride in silence for what seems to be several hours.

When the blindfold is removed, you find yourself in a small cabin. You look out the window and discover that you are deep in a forest.

Three men wearing white robes are standing around a small card table staring at the diamond. The men have long, white beards and wear turbans. One of them still holds a blowgun in one hand. They seem too busy staring at the diamond to notice you studying them.

What do they want the diamond for? What do they plan to do to you?

Turn to PAGE 24.

You leap into your house and slam the front door behind you. You gasp for breath. You've never run so fast in your life. You can hear the creatures running around in your front yard. But they don't seem to be coming up to the front door—yet.

"Is that you?" Uncle Clyde calls. He's sitting in his armchair in the living room reading a newspaper.

"Yes—it's—me," you manage to wheeze.

"Hey—didja see the Grover twins from down the street in their costumes?" Uncle Clyde asks. "Funniest costumes I ever saw. Like two purple tomatoes with legs! They've got their own inflatable flying saucer, too. Didja see them?"

"Uh—no, no I didn't," you lie. "Sounds great."

You feel like a total fool.

The Grover twins will be laughing at you for the rest of your life. How mortifying!

If only you could run away.

Hey—maybe you can!

"Uncle Clyde, I've got a great idea on how to spend the million dollars," you say. "Let's take a trip around the world!"

"Okay," Uncle Clyde says. "I've got a coupla weeks' vacation coming. Let's go! Shall we go by plane or by ship?"

It's your choice.

Plane? Turn to PAGE 14.
Ship? Turn to PAGE 80.

You lead the two purple creatures to your house. Luckily, Uncle Clyde is at work. You're not quite sure how you'd explain your two visitors to him.

"Money! Money! Money!" they continue chanting, following you as you go to your room and bring out the box containing the thousand thousand dollar bills.

You stack the money on the dining room table, and the two creatures draw close. One of them picks up a thousand dollar bill and stuffs it hungrily into its mouth. Then the other one eats a thousand dollar bill, chewing it greedily, making a loud "gulp" as it swallows your money.

In less than five minutes, the two creatures have eaten the entire million dollars!

You are too horrified to move, too shocked to speak. They give you several pats on the back with their many arms and race out the door, their dinner completed.

You sit staring at the empty dining room table for a long while. Then you realize that maybe this was a lucky break. After all, you did give away the million dollars!

"Yes! Yes! I've done it!" you cry aloud. "I'm entitled to the five million!"

Yes, you *are* entitled to it. But of course you have one small problem: Just how good do you think the chances are that Mr. Vandermint will believe your story???

THE END

You decide that spending all the money on yourself is pretty boring. "Know what I'm going to do with it?" you tell your friends. "I'm going to build the greatest amusement park ever built — right here in this town! We'll never be bored again!"

Your friends begin to cheer up immediately. Everyone agrees that it's a wonderful idea.

You begin at once to get the amusement park designed and built. You hire the best architects you can find. You make sure the park is filled with all of the greatest rides, dozens of interesting shows, animated monsters and dinosaurs, hamburger restaurants, and places to swim and play all kinds of sports.

By the end of the month, you have spent the million dollars. And you keep right on spending until the next five million has gone into the park, too. It's going to be the most exciting, most lavish, most eye-popping amusement park in the world!

Are you ready for opening day?

Go to PAGE 47.

You walk as fast as you can toward Andy's house. You turn your head quickly to see if the man is still following.

Yes! He's walking as fast as you.

You begin to run. You run across the street. A truck squeals to a halt. "Hey, kid — watch where you're goin'!" the driver screams angrily.

But you keep running. Andy's house is just two houses away now. You turn back. Has the man crossed the street? Yes. He's walking toward you, walking quickly, steadily, silently toward you.

You run up the drive to Andy's house. The front door is closed. You pound on the door as hard as you can. You pound desperately, your heart racing in your chest.

"Come on, somebody! Somebody open up!" you cry. You pound with both fists.

The man is at Andy's driveway now. "Please! Somebody! Open up!" you cry. There's no one home. You'll have to make a run for it. You turn to see how close the man is.

He has walked on past Andy's house. He turns the corner and disappears from view.

He wasn't following you after all.

Having a million dollars can make you pretty jumpy, can't it?

Better cool out for a while. Take a short rest before turning to PAGE 12.

The fanciest car showroom in town is filled with sleek sports cars. You and Uncle Clyde look at all of them, and you test-drive the fanciest, most expensive ones.

"Aren't you the kid who won the million dollar lottery?" the salesman asks. "I'm so glad you decided to spend your money here."

"Me, too," you say. "I'll take one of those and one of those and one of those and one of those."

"Save a little money," Uncle Clyde says. "I want to buy a Chevy to drive to work."

A few minutes later, you are seated beside Uncle Clyde as he drives your new $60,000 Lambaglorioso sports car. You feel great! You've spent all of the money. You're going to have the most valuable collection of new sports cars in the state!

You are almost home when you spot the little man in the black frock coat on the sidewalk. He is between two policemen, who are pulling him roughly toward their car.

"Stop the car!" you cry to your uncle. "That's the man who delivered the money to me. Let's see why he's in trouble."

Why *is* he in trouble with the police?

Turn to PAGE 41.

"What do you mean there are no hamburgers? We're starving!" you cry.

"Somethin' wrong with these new stoves," Uncle Clyde explains, his tools spread all over the floor.

"Well, let's not waste time here, guys," you say, pulling your friends away from the hamburger stand. "Let's try the Prehistoric Boat Ride."

You pull them into the dark tunnel that houses the Prehistoric Boat Ride, and you all climb into the log canoe that will carry you on your journey, back, back — into *total darkness!*

"Uh . . . we seem to have a power failure," you say glumly.

"How do we get outta here?!" Andy cries. "It's pitch black!"

"We're stuck here in the middle of the water!" Jack yells.

"The water is only two feet deep," you tell them. "Jump out of the boat. We can wade to the exit."

You all jump into the cold, dark water. "Which way is the exit?" Andy asks.

No one is sure.

You wade around in the dark for what seems like hours. Finally, lights go on. The canoe starts up again. But it's going ten times faster than normal and its heading right *at you!!*

Turn to PAGE 83.

A few moments later, the sales clerk returns carrying a tray of gleaming diamonds. He sets the tray down gently on the counter in front of you. "If you'd care to take a look at these," he says softly.

You look down at the dazzling array of diamonds. They all look the same to you — except for one. One of the diamonds casts a blue-white light that seems to signal to you. You can't take your eyes off it.

"I'll take that one," you say, your voice trembling.

"Oh, no! Not that one!" the sales clerk cries. "Please — don't buy that one. That diamond has a curse on it!"

"Ha ha! A curse?!" you exclaim. "Come on — don't be so corny!"

"This is an ancient diamond that just happens to come with an ancient curse," the clerk insists, holding onto the countertop tightly. "I'd really advise you not to buy this one."

You stare down at the beautiful jewel. You feel drawn to it, pulled into it, hypnotized by it.

You must decide. Will you buy it despite the curse?

Or will you decide not to take the chance — in case a curse really exists — and buy something else?

Buy the diamond? Turn to PAGE 44.
Don't buy it? Turn to PAGE 87.

You turn and run from the approaching purple creatures. Your house is just half a block away. Can you get there and lock the door before they catch up to you?

Their arms wave wildly in the air as they chase after you. Their four heads bob up and down on their necks.

They're getting closer. You've got to run faster!

Just a few more yards and you'll be home!

Will you get there? And can you keep these weird creatures out?!

Turn to PAGE 52.

You run through the crowd, squeeze your way up to the stage, and take the microphone. "Ladies and gentlemen, the circus is about to begin."

"Wait a minute! Just a minute!" cries a voice behind you. It's Mr. McKeevy, the town mayor! What does *he* want?

He takes the microphone away from you and begins a speech, thanking you for throwing the party. He thanks you for twenty minutes as you stand behind him, growing more and more embarrassed. "Finally, I just want to say that the people of this town didn't think it fair for you to pay for this wonderful party," the mayor yells. "We took up a collection. Everyone in town donated ten dollars, and I'm happy to say we have $300,000 for you."

The crowd cheers, the entire park in one enormous, ear-shattering roar. "Oh, no, oh, no!" you moan to yourself. "I'm going to make a *profit* on this party! I just know it!"

"And I have more good news!" the mayor cries.

You don't know how much more good news you can take!

"The Cadillac dealer in town has volunteered to donate all of the Cadillac door prizes! They won't cost you a penny!"

Again, the huge crowd roars.

Will there be more "good" news?

Go on to PAGE 61.

Before the mayor can make any more announcements, there is a flash of lightning, followed by a barrage of thunder, and the rain begins to pour down. People run to the small shelters that dot the park. Others put up umbrellas or hold newspapers over their heads. It is a downpour.

"Excuse me," calls a timid voice to the side of the stage. It is the man who runs the fireworks show.

"I am so sorry," he tells you. "But the fireworks just got all wet in this downpour. They won't dry out for days, maybe weeks. We'll have to cancel. You'll get a full refund, of course."

He turns and walks away into the rain.

There is another flash of lightning, then another.

You hear the frightened trumpeting of elephants. And then, through the pouring rain, you see that the elephants have *escaped!*

With a sound like thunder, their heavy feet pound the rain-soaked ground as they flee in terror, at least ten frightened elephants. They're heading right toward the center of town!

"Great news!" you tell yourself. "They'll do a million dollars in damages! I'll have to pay! It's probably the only thing I'll get to pay for today!!"

Turn to PAGE 67.

You run through the woods, your heart pounding so loudly you can't hear the footsteps behind you. Without stopping, you drop the bag containing the diamond into the trunk of the hollow tree. You keep running, darting through the tangled trees.

Are they still following you?

Are they right behind you?

CRAAAAAACK!

Suddenly you see the blue-white light of the diamond, glowing brighter, brighter. Then the glow fades and everything goes black.

Turn to PAGE 70.

You step forward bravely and raise your hand in greeting. The two creatures stop in front of you. All four of their mouths seem to be smiling. Does this mean they're friendly?

One of them reaches into a pouch in its chest. "What is it reaching for?" you ask yourself. "Some sort of blaster ray gun to blow me to smithereens?" You take a step back.

The creature pulls a book out of its pouch.

It holds the book up to its face and searches through the pages. You can read the title on the front: *Kwellian-English/English-Kwellian Dictionary.*

The creature is going to try to speak to you in English. You can't wait! What will be the first words from a creature from another planet?

"Take me to your money!" it says.

Turn to PAGE 45.

"I can't believe it! No one believes me!" you say to yourself. "Maybe it's too dark here in this corner and people can't see that I'm offering real money."

You move to a brightly lit area in front of a restaurant. Two men in loud plaid suits come walking up to you.

"Say, what are you doing here?" one of them asks with a wide grin. He winks at his companion.

"Yes, what are you doing here?" the other one repeats, nudging his companion in the ribs with his elbow.

"What's with these two jerks?" you ask yourself. You hold up a wad of thousand dollar bills. "I'm trying to give away money," you say.

For some reason these two men find your answer simply hilarious. They laugh uproariously, slapping their knees and poking each other, winking and grinning.

"This is an exciting moment!" the first one cries, nudging his partner.

"Right you are!" cries his partner, winking and grinning.

"Uh-oh," you say. "Something funny is going on here."

Go on to PAGE 65.

"Come on, you son of a gun! You recognize us!" cries the first grinning man. He puts a hand on your shoulder and spins you around. You find yourself staring into a TV camera. No wonder the lights were so bright here!

"You know who we are?" cries the second one. "We're Eddie and Freddie Giveaway! And you are on live TV! You're on *Win A Million* — and we're going to give you a million dollars just for being such a good sport!"

"Oh, no! Oh, no!" you cry.

"Another happy winner!" cries Eddie (or is it Freddie?). "Look at our winner — actual tears, folks! Ha ha!"

THE END

You rush down to the speedway to talk with the manager. With the party just two days away, you've got to find a place to hold it — fast!

The stock car races are in progress, a dozen cars roaring around the track. You find the manager in the pit. He's a short, stocky guy with a stubby black mustache that looks as if it was glued under his nose.

"I need to talk to you about renting the speedway," you tell him.

"What?" he cries, trying to hear you over the roar of the racing cars.

"I'm giving a party for the whole town. I want to rent the speedway."

"What?"

"Is the speedway for rent?"

"You what? You want to place a bet?" he asks. "There's no betting here. Scram!"

"Not *bet*. Rent. RENT!" you scream.

"Listen, I can't hear you. I got earplugs in my ears because of the noise!" he screams. "Why don't you write me a letter?" He turns back to watch the cars.

It looks as if you'll just have to hold your party in the park — the *free* park. Maybe you'll think of another way you can spend the money that would have gone for rent.

Turn to PAGE 11.

A few hours later, drenched from the rain, so tired and depressed you can barely stand up, you and Uncle Clyde head for home.

"Too bad about the elephants," Uncle Clyde says quietly. "They sure did a lot of damage in town."

"But it was all covered by the circus's insurance," you say sadly. "I didn't pay for a thing, not a thing."

"How badly did you do?" your uncle asks, sympathetic for the first time.

You do some fast figuring in your head.

"I made a profit of $14," you tell him.

"Not bad. Not bad," he says, chuckling. "Tell you what. I'll let you spend that $14 on me — okay?"

"Okay," you say.

"Let's go have a coupla pizzas!" says Uncle Clyde.

THE END

"What are you selling?" the man asks as you walk up and say hello. He's wearing a light-blue suit that fits a bit too snugly around his large waist. He squints down at you as if he has trouble with his eyes.

"I hope you'll believe me," you begin timidly. "I'm not selling anything. I'd like to give you this thousand dollar bill. It's absolutely free. Please take it."

The man takes the bill from you. He holds it up close to his face and squints at it for a long time. "Good detail," he says finally. He hands it back to you.

"What?" you ask. What is he talking about?

"Not a bad job, actually," the man says, searching in his jacket pocket for something. "It's really one of the best bills I've seen. But the background is a bit murky. Here — take a look at one of mine."

He hands you a thousand dollar bill.

Is he saying that your money is counterfeit?

Go on to PAGE 69.

"See? I use a higher grade ink than you do," he says with pride. "It makes the background come up sharper."

You stare in disbelief at the phony bill in your hand.

"You can keep that one." the man says. He walks off and disappears into a store.

"He *can't* be right!" you tell yourself. "My money *can't* be counterfeit!"

You put his bill in your pocket and take out one of yours. You examine it carefully. First the front, then the back.

On the back of the bill, at the bottom, in tiny, tiny type, you read the words: "Otto Quincy Vandermint Practical Joke Company."

What a hilarious joke!!

So why aren't you laughing?

THE END

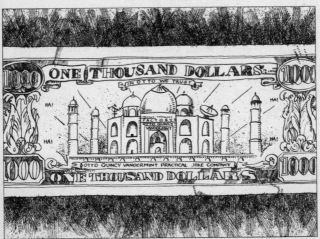

"Hey — we're sorry," a voice cries. "We didn't mean to hurt you — honest!"

You try to focus your eyes. It isn't easy. Your head throbs. The pain goes all the way down to your knees.

"Are you okay? We didn't mean to hurt you," the small, scared voice repeats.

You look up to see two of the neighborhood kids peering down at you. You try to get up from the ground, but you're too dizzy.

"The blowguns?" you ask, struggling to clear your head. "The poison darts?"

You see that the two boys are carrying slingshots.

"We were just playing," one of them says, tears welling up in his eyes. "We didn't mean for you to run into that tree."

You feel your forehead. There's a bump on it the size of a cantaloupe!

"I'm okay, you guys," you say, getting up slowly.

"Hey — where you going?" one of the kids asks. "You better take care of that bump on your head."

"I will," you say, "but there's something I've got to take care of first."

Go on to PAGE 71.

"I knew it. I knew it," the jewelry store owner says as you walk back into his store. "I knew you'd be back with that cursed diamond. Everyone who owns that diamond runs into trouble!"

"Actually, I ran into a tree," you say, supressing a laugh.

"But you came back! You want to return the diamond before the curse ruins your life!"

"I do want to return the diamond," you tell him. "But not because of the curse. I've decided I don't want diamonds or other unimportant things. I want to spend my fortune on things of true value — things with substance and meaning. Things that will improve the quality of life and bring happiness to a suffering world . . ."

"Really?" The store owner is impressed. "What do you plan to do?"

"Well . . . how long do you think it will take to spend a million dollars on chocolate bars?"

THE END

Giving a party is always difficult. Giving a party for 30,000 people is next to impossible!

You spend the next few weeks running all over town, making arrangements, buying supplies, getting organized.

You hire people to send out 30,000 invitations. You spend $100,000 renting the Civic Auditorium. It should be just big enough to hold the party.

You order pepperoni pizza for 30,000 people. Then you remember that some people may prefer sausage. So you order enough sausage pizza for 30,000 people — just to be safe!

You hire ten different bands to play. You order a thousand door prizes — new-model Cadillacs! You spend, spend, spend. Can you spend a million dollars on this party?

You're doing your very best!

"How's it goin'?" your uncle asks, his face buried in the newspaper.

"I can't talk now," you tell him. "I'm on the phone with the fireworks people. They want to put on a $100,000 show. I'm trying to talk them into something more expensive!"

"That's nice," Uncle Clyde says. He didn't hear a word you said.

The party is only two days away. Will it be a success?

Turn to PAGE 90.

The three men continue to stare at the diamond, transfixed by its blue-white beauty. Silently, you get up from your chair in the corner of the room. They were so eager to enjoy their prize, they didn't even bother to tie you up.

And now, they don't see you as you make your way to the door of the cabin, silently open it just wide enough to get through, and dash into the woods . . .

. . . into the arms of a *fourth* robed man standing guard outside!

Turn to PAGE 34.

You don't drive this car — you aim it! Without even putting your foot on the gas, you find yourself going 80 m.p.h. through town.

In a few minutes you are out on the highway, farms and fields flying by you. You look down at the speedometer. You are doing 150 m.p.h. and the car glides as smoothly as if you were doing 35!

You turn it around and head back to town. People along the road stop and stare as you whiz by. Soon, the showroom comes into view. You put your foot down gently on the brake.

Nothing happens.

You push a little harder on the brake.

The car doesn't slow down a bit!

You push the brake all the way down.

Nothing!

The brakes do not work. You speed through town and are back on the highway. You can't seem to get the car to slow down — forget stopping!

What will you do now — jump out, or try to stay with it and slow it down?

If you choose to jump out, turn to PAGE 81.

If you think you'd better stay in the car and try to bring it to a stop, turn to PAGE 18.

Good luck!

CONGRATULATIONS!!!
Number 13 is a lucky number for you.
You are the grand-prize winner.
You are an INSTANT MILLIONAIRE!

In a few moments, you will be handed one million dollars in cash! But hold on — don't rush out to start buying your weight in candy bars and comic books. There are some special rules to the INSTANT MILLIONAIRE lottery — special rules that you'd better learn.

Turn to PAGE 6 for your special instructions.

The creatures climb slowly out of the saucer-shaped craft. They stretch their six arms. They look all around with their two heads.

You look for a place to hide.

But it's too late. One of them sees you. It begins to point with three of its arms.

The two weird creatures begin to run toward you.

What an amazing experience! You could be the first person on Earth to have contact with creatures from another planet!

Should you step forward and greet them?

Or should you run away?

You'll have to decide fast. Their little legs are carrying them quickly toward you!

Do you choose to greet them? Turn to PAGE 63.

Do you choose to play it safe and run for your house? Turn to PAGE 59.

"No one will believe me if I just stand here waving money in the air," you tell yourself. "I'll pick out some likely looking prospects and go up and talk to them."

You stand and watch the people pass by for a moment. You see a teenager looking at watches in the window of a drugstore. You see a young mother arguing with her five-year-old daughter about which direction to take. And you see a well-dressed, middle-aged man walking aimlessly, obviously just window-shopping.

Surely, one of these three people will gladly take some free money from you and start you on your way to getting rid of the million dollars. But which one?

Do you choose the teenager? Turn to PAGE 28.

Do you choose the young mother? Turn to PAGE 48.

Do you choose the middle-aged man? Turn to PAGE 68.

The Broadway musical goes on as scheduled, and the gigantic crowd loves every minute of it. While the play is on, you frantically call every restaurant in all of the nearby towns and ask them to deliver everything on their menus — as much as they can get to you in the next two hours.

An hour later, trucks filled with all sorts of food begin to pull into the park. After the play, the entire town enjoys lunch.

Then the professional rodeo begins. What a thrill as the hundreds of cowboys you've invited compete for the $300,000 prize!

The party continues on PAGE 86.

The beautiful luxury oceanliner, the S.S. *Penguin*, sets sail for London. You stand on the first-class deck and watch the busy port disappear in the distance. The cry of gulls follows the ship for a while, then fades as the majestic birds turn and glide back to land. You are at sea. The whole world lies ahead of you.

"Let's go get a root beer," says Uncle Clyde.

"How about a root beer float?" you suggest. "Remember, we're going first class all the way!"

The ocean journey is beautiful and calm — for about three days.

Then a fierce, battering storm comes up. The gigantic ship could handle the storm easily — except that it develops engine trouble. To save power, the captain shuts down the electricity. And since the ship has electric heat, the temperature on board soon dips to 30 degrees!

"Can anything else go wrong?" you ask your uncle.

Turn to PAGE 93.

"I can't stop this car!" you tell yourself. "I've got to jump out!"

You pull the car into a grassy field. You struggle to get the door open. The handle is stuck. You give it a tug. Another tug. Finally the door opens. You jump —

— and you find yourself floating in a black sky.

Stars twinkle past as you fall, down, down, past the moon, past Saturn with its rings. . . . You fall down, down, down . . .

. . . till you land in your own bed.

You sit up and look around.

"I've been dreaming," you say aloud. "Wow! What a ride!"

Was this dream trying to tell you *not* to go shopping for cars?

If you believe it was, *why not go shopping for diamonds instead? Turn to PAGE 40.*

If you are still determined to spend your million on cars, turn to PAGE 56.

You duck underwater and the motorized canoe speeds past, missing you by inches. Your friends duck out of the way, too — and now you're all swimming and spluttering toward the exit.

You're soaking wet and shivering from the cold. "Let's go into the World of the Sun to warm up," you suggest.

But the door to World of the Sun has been stuck all day, and no one can get in. "Don't worry, gang, we'll get the bugs out. "Hey — what's that rumbling sound?"

It's the animated dinosaurs! They've escaped! Somehow they've broken out of their exhibit hall, and they're marching down the center lane of the park! "Look out! They weigh two tons!" you cry.

People are fleeing for their lives. The air is filled with cries of terror. You see your friends leap out of the way as the mechanized dinosaurs stampede through the park.

A while later, you are outside the gate of your park, apologizing to your friends. You struggle to be heard over the sirens of fire trucks and ambulances.

"That was the greatest!" Andy cries. "The most exciting park I've ever been to!"

"Parks that work right are so boring!" Jack agrees. "We'll all meet here tomorrow and do it again. And whatever you do — don't fix anything!!"

THE END

You walk until you get to the corner, picking up speed, walking as fast as you can. You turn to see that the man is still the same distance behind you.

You turn the corner onto the street the school is on. You begin to run now. You run without looking back, but you can hear the man's footsteps behind you. He is now running, too!

You're breathing hard as you reach the playground. Your mouth is dry, your chest is heaving as you gasp for air. You run right through a baseball game. "Hey — watch where you're goin'!" some kid yells angrily as you cross over second base.

You turn to see if the man is still following you.

Yes. He's running at full speed now, his dark coat flapping behind him. He's getting closer!

It's a hundred yards or so to the school building. You know you'll be safe if you can get inside. You're almost there! You've almost made it!

— But — look out!! — you trip over a softball someone left in the grass. You sprawl forward on the ground. The man is right behind you!

Go on to PAGE 85.

The man stands above you as you struggle to your feet. Your heart is pounding, your head is throbbing. You feel too dizzy to stand.

"I'm terribly sorry to trouble you," the man says in a clipped British accent. You suddenly realize it is the little man who gave you your prize money.

"Could you please sign on the line here? I'm afraid I forgot to get a receipt!"

Sure, you feel a little silly making him run three blocks to get your signature. But a million dollars is bound to make you act a little weird, don't you think?

Go ahead. Sign the receipt. Catch your breath. Then turn to PAGE 12.

After the rodeo, the air show featuring nearly 500 planes thrills the crowd. Everyone also loves the water ballet, which takes place in the immense lake you had dug in the center of the park just for this occasion. The professional soccer match featuring the two best teams of Europe is also a hit. And the party is capped off by the three-hour fireworks show in which nearly a half-million dollars' worth of fireworks are set off.

"I think the party was a success," you tell Uncle Clyde as the crowds begin to head for home a little after midnight.

But did you manage to spend the million dollars?

Turn to PAGE 88.

"Well, I guess you're right," you tell the clerk. "With my luck, there probably *is* a curse on the diamond, and some ancient, smelly mummy will stagger after me for the rest of my life, trying to get the diamond back! Let's skip it."

"May I show you some emeralds or rubies?" the clerk asks. "Most of them don't have curses on them."

"I think maybe this whole thing is a mistake," you tell him. "I'm going out to spend this million on things that are more fun than jewels! I'm going to go on the biggest shopping spree this town has ever seen! I'm going to buy at least one of everything in town!"

To begin your shopping spree, turn to PAGE 35.

At one o'clock in the morning, you are still in the communications tent in the park. Working under the bright spotlights you had installed for the party, Uncle Clyde is still adding up the bills.

Finally, he turns to you. He yawns. Once. Twice. Then he says, "You did it! You spent the whole million!"

"YAAAAAAAAAY!" you cry, jumping up and down even though you're completely exhausted.

"And — " Uncle Clyde says.

"And? And?" you cry. "And what?" This "and" is making you nervous!

"And, I'm sorry to say . . ." your uncle says slowly.

"Sorry?! Sorry?! What?!"

". . . that you seem to have spent a total of . . . five million more. The party cost exactly six million dollars!"

THE END

"It's the police!" you cry, opening the door. Four policemen burst into the room. They rush forward to take the three robed men prisoners.

"Congratulations," a familiar voice calls from the doorway. The clerk from the diamond store has accompanied the police. "These men have been trying to steal the diamond for many years. It doesn't belong to their country, and it never did. Thanks to you, they have been captured. The curse on the diamond has been removed. *They* were the curse — and now they will be behind bars."

"But, but — the diamond was only glass!" you cry, still in a state of shock.

"I gave you a fake," the clerk says. "I'm not really a salesman. I'm an FBI agent. I've been working with the local police to capture these men. Once we gave you the fake diamond, we had you followed. We hoped something like this would happen."

"And the real diamond?" you ask.

"It is safe in the store's vault. It's there waiting for you. *And* you'll be getting a very large reward for the capture of these men."

You are too exhausted to smile.

"What do you plan to spend the reward money on?" the FBI man asks.

You don't have to think before you answer. "Anything but diamonds!!"

THE END

The phone rings. You pick it up. "This is Mr. Harris at the Civic Auditorium," a voice says. "I'm afraid I have bad news."

"What's the problem?" you ask. "You don't have enough ice buckets to hold 20,000 tons of ice?"

"No," he answers. "I'm afraid it's a bit more serious than that. I'm afraid we have a bit of a conflict. You won't be able to use the Civic Auditorium after all."

"What? What?" you scream, losing your cool. *"The party is in two days!!"*

"I'm so sorry," Mr. Harris says quietly. "But we realized yesterday that we had rented the auditorium for that day for the all-city string quintet tryouts. They reserved months ago, so we have to honor their reservation."

"What am I supposed to do?" you cry.

But he has hung up.

You realize there are only two other places where you could hold such a large party. At the speedway, where the stock-car races are held. Or at the municipal park in the center of town. The park is free, which is a real disadvantage. You had hoped to spend a lot of your money renting the space for the party. The speedway is very run-down.

Which will it be?

The speedway? Turn to PAGE 66.
The park? Turn to PAGE 11.

"Gettin' mighty windy out there," Uncle Clyde says cheerfully when you get off the phone. You stare out of the tent at the huge crowd filling the park. You don't know how you're going to announce to them that there won't be any food at this party!

"It's goin' to rain before you know it," Uncle Clyde says. "Better get the entertainment on early."

The entertainment! Right! Good idea. Now . . . which entertainment did you finally decide on for this party? The Broadway play with the original Broadway cast? Or the three-ring circus?

The Broadway play? Turn to PAGE 79.
The circus? Turn to PAGE 60.

You walk the few blocks back to your house. "I never dreamed it would be this hard to give away money," you tell yourself.

Half a block from your house, you see something that makes you forget about your million dollars. Are your eyes playing tricks on you? Are you really watching two large, purple creatures climbing out of a low, saucer-shaped vehicle?

Turn to PAGE 76.

The ship's engines go out completely. Repair crews work around the clock, but with no success. The ship drifts aimlessly, first north, then west.

The weather turns colder. Fights break out among the angry passengers.

And then disaster strikes!

The ship has drifted north into frozen waters. It crashes into a giant ice mass. And it sticks.

Days pass. "Rescue ships are on the way," the Captain assures everyone. But more days pass, and no ships appear on the horizon.

You realize that time is running out. The month is almost over — and there's no way you'll be able to spend the million dollars while you're stranded aboard this ship.

"I've failed," you tell yourself. "I can't believe it. The lucky break of a lifetime. And I completely blew it!"

Cheer up. Things are going to get worse.

Turn to PAGE 17.

Collect All the Twistaplot® Books

An old book you buy at a tag sale makes you the master of the magical arts. Will you use your power for revenge? Will you transform yourself into a hero? And will you escape the witches and wizards who envy your power?